T0113861

THE
STAR
RADIO SHOW

A Christmas Program

Leigh Ellen Carson

WESTBOW
PRESS®
A DIVISION OF THOMAS NELSON
& ZONDERVAN

WestBow Press books may be ordered through booksellers or by contacting:

WestBow Press
A Division of Thomas Nelson & Zondervan
1663 Liberty Drive
Bloomington, IN 47403
www.westbowpress.com
844-714-3454

Because of the dynamic nature of the Internet, any web addresses or
links contained in this book may have changed since publication and
may no longer be valid. The views expressed in this work are solely those
of the author and do not necessarily reflect the views of the publisher,
and the publisher hereby disclaims any responsibility for them.

Any people depicted in stock imagery provided by Getty Images are models,
and such images are being used for illustrative purposes only.
Certain stock imagery © Getty Images.

ISBN: 978-1-6642-7809-7 (sc)
ISBN: 978-1-6642-7808-0 (e)

Print information available on the last page.

WestBow Press rev. date: 10/19/2022

Thank you to Drew Carson for being the "STAR" of the cover photo.

To my mom, Marijke, who dreamed up and
wrote stellar Christmas Programs for years.
Thank you for setting the standard
that homemade is always best.

The STAR Radio Show:
A Youth Christmas Vignette in Two Acts
with 2 male, 12 non-gendered, and 7 extra roles

CHARACTERS *(To adapt the number of roles, see the Production Notes at back of the script.):*

HAPPY HIGHMORE: Host of STAR Radio. Diligent about work. All around grump, especially at Christmas time.

JACK ALONZO: Co-host of STAR Radio. Eternal optimist. Sees potential in any and everything.

THE SIMPLE SHEPHERDS (5 Roles: 3 Shepherds, 2 Sheep): Your average hipster coffee house band. Dedicated to the uncomplicated things in life, but recently inspired to spread a global message.

KINGS AND CAMELS (8 Roles: 3 Kings, 5 Gift Bearers): Rock and roll. Or rather, rock and *rule*. Stoic and serious, but incredibly generous.

THE LITTLE ANGEL BAND (4 Roles: 4 Angels): A traveling a cappella family group eager to add more members and encourage those who need it most.

SOUND EFFECTS (SFX): In charge of all sounds during commercials.

CONTROL BOARD OPERATOR (CBO): In charge of the microphones and 'ON AIR' sign.

ADVERTISING MANAGER (AD. MAN.): In charge of rotating advertising signs and roster board.

TIME: Late 1940s, Christmas Eve

PLACE: Any standard city large enough to warrant a radio station.

SETTING: The entire vignette takes place in the studio of STAR Radio, a tight yet cozy room. It follows the story of a Scrooge-like radio host who falls asleep mid-show and is visited by three musical guests, all with a part of the Christmas story to share. There should be space for a control booth/station, a sound effects table and microphone, a coat and hat stand, and a small desk and office chair for the host, littered with newspaper and a few forgotten coffee mugs. The scene should have an 'organized clutter' feel of a studio where radio theatre takes place. Discarded pages on the ground, various sound effect props scattered about, microphones and wires, an 'ON AIR' sign, a rug or two. Christmas decorations may be featured, although kept to a minimum. Microphone and music stand usage and placement will be important also, stage permitting.

<u>Note</u>: *See Production Notes at the end of the script for additional and more detailed staging options.*

SIGNS OR POSTERS: Typical of many radio shows of the time, commercials were lively and frequent. Throughout the show several advertisements will be featured. These are based on actual radio commercial jingles and include both sound effects and a sign or poster featured in the studio (for the audience's benefit). There are three commercials in this script, and each should have an eye-catching poster or sign made to go with it to be displayed on easels. Ad. Man. can rotate these signs as each new commercial is announced.

COSTUMES, LIGHTS, PROPS, SOUND EFFECTS, and MUSIC: Any part not assigned to one of the musical guests should be costumed in period clothing (1940s). If full costuming isn't possible, good dress clothes will work with a few key pieces of the day: fedoras, suspenders and ties, neck scarves, white hand gloves, etc. For THE SIMPLE SHEPHERDS, inspiration may be borrowed from folk bands (except for the Sheep, who should be dressed, well, like sheep). For KINGS AND CAMELS, go nuts with 80's rock and roll gear: teased hair, neon colors, fingerless gloves, leather anything. THE LITTLE ANGEL BAND should be decked out in white or gold clothing. As this is a version of a nativity play, nods to the traditional roles in the story may be used: a staff for the shepherds, crowns for the kings, halos for the angels, etc.

If possible, dim lights in the audience so wherever this is performed may have a 'stage-like' effect. This is one element of the show where simple is easiest. A few strings of Christmas lights will add enough of an atmosphere. Prop requirements are relatively minimal as it's all about the set dressing. Things needed: any sound effect items, instruments for band members, wrapped presents for the Gift Bearers with Kings and Camels, and a nativity set. Anything else is up to the imagination of the director!

Sound effects (SFX) are featured heavily in this show. In the script it is written as one person but having a team of SFX artists is a great way to incorporate kids who are uncomfortable with speaking roles (or any older kids needing a volunteer position). This role does require some good comedic timing, so practicing with props will be necessary! All SFX props/usage will be labeled [**SFX: ...**] in the script, so take note on what may be needed.

Music should be one of the larger focuses of the vignette. Carols have been pre-selected for this show but are certainly not set in stone. If a youth program has a particular favorite, minor tweaking to the script can accommodate that. All youth involved should join in on the singing as well as any audience members in attendance. At the 'intermission' is a great place to feature some musical talent. If there are any youth (or adults at a pinch) who play an instrument, having them share their gift is a wonderful addition to the show. Another option would be to have the youth join their church choir for an Advent-themed song.

STYLE/PACING: As many involved in youth programming will know, nothing ever goes as planned. This show is designed to get a laugh, so coaching kids on how to wait until people are done laughing before continuing with their lines is important. Run time on this show is about 20 minutes without music, but this is not a professional production! If it takes an extra couple of minutes because the five-year-old sheep wanders out into the audience and the shepherds must go get them (which happened during the inaugural production of this show), relax and have fun! This story is about the hope of Jesus' birth, a message of good news and great joy. Let it be glad.

PROLOGUE

[A suggested use of a playlist consisting of Christmas crooner classics and old radio jingles should be played (see Production Notes) as the audience takes their seats. It fades out and HAPPY HIGHMORE enters, grouchy and dejected. He hangs up his coat and hat.]

HAPPY HIGHMORE: I can't believe I'm working on Christmas Eve. It's the one time of year that everyone should have off so they can relax and I'm going to be sitting here all night, broadcasting music in an empty studio until the crack of dawn. No place like home for the holidays, huh? What's the point? Most of my family is too far away to visit and decorating a house for just one person doesn't sound festive at all. Maybe that Scrooge fellow was right about all that Bah Humbug stuff.

[HAPPY begins his radio show on his own, fiddling with the control board and turning on the ON AIR sign. He does his

1

best to muster up an energetic voice and attitude. His listeners still deserve a night of entertainment.]

HAPPY *(cont'd)*: Good evening, ladies and gentlemen, and welcome to STAR Radio's Christmas extravaganza where the songs keep flowing just like the eggnog! I'm your host, Happy Highmore! We'll kick things off this evening with a little [insert artist and song here, something akin to Perry Como or Frank Sinatra].

[As the song begins, HAPPY reverts to his grumbly self. It's late and he yawns or stretches and takes a seat at his desk chair. Slowly, he nods off… and the dream world begins.]

SCENE ONE

"WHAT SHOW?"

[After a beat of some light snoring from HAPPY, the song fades out and JACK ALONZO enters followed by SFX, AD. MAN., and CBO. After seeing HAPPY asleep and chuckling with his pals, JACK clears his throat.]

JACK ALONZO *(loudly)*: Well, if it isn't Happy Highmore. Radio host extraordinaire and my favorite boss.

HAPPY *(startled)*: I'm your only boss, Jack.

JACK: That's right! So don't fire me because STAR Radio is my life. And it also pays the bills.

HAPPY *(grouchy again, now that he's awake)*: Why are you here, Jack?

JACK: You told us to come in, don't you remember? After all, we've got a big show tonight. Three special guests who have very important messages to share.

HAPPY: What?! I thought it was just me playing Christmas records.

JACK: Nope! Look at the roster board, boss.

[AD. MAN. reveals a letter display or chalk board with THE SIMPLE SHEPHERDS, KINGS AND CAMELS, and THE LITTLE ANGEL BAND written on it in that order.]

HAPPY: Who are these people? The Simple Shepherds? Kings and Camels? The Little Angel Band?

JACK *(shrugging)*: I dunno. You picked 'em.

[SFX, AD. MAN., and CBO all take their places and go through the motions of setting up for the show. They may have fun with the audience a little, testing SFX props, handing out flyers for commercials, or testing microphones.]

JACK *(cont'd.)*: Okay, boss, we better get started.

[JACK leads a bewildered HAPPY to their places behind microphones. CBO flicks three, two, one with their fingers and turns on the ON AIR sign.]

JACK *(cont'd.)*: And we're back! I'm Jack Alonzo here with Happy Highmore. Guys and gals, before we continue with our Christmas Eve special, a little word from our sponsors.

[AD. MAN. reveals a poster for Sparkle and Shine, a toothpaste company.]

JACK *(cont'd.)*: For the safety of your smile, use Sparkle and Shine Toothpaste! **[SFX: Bell ring.]** That's right, I get paid to talk about Sparkle and Shine, but you folks are the people who really collect. All you have to do is brush your teeth with that fresh mint paste **[SFX: Brush bristles.]** to remove that film that makes your teeth all dingy. You could have a bright smile that could dazzle every dance floor and not even know it! Pick up a tube of Sparkle and Shine Toothpaste and sparkle once again! **[SFX: Bell ring.]** Now, onto our first guest, The Simple Shepherds! **[SFX: Applause.]**

SCENE TWO

"BAA HUMBUG"

[THE SIMPLE SHEPHERDS, consisting of three 'shepherds' and two sheep enter. They are jolly and equipped with traditional folk instruments, e.g., a guitar, a mandolin, spoons, recorder, ukulele, an accordion for fancier productions. Instruments can be cardboard/toy or real (although education on care will be required). They smile and wave to those in the radio station and the audience]

HAPPY *(thoroughly confused)*: Um, hello. Welcome to STAR radio. Who are you again?

SHEPHERD 1: We're The Simple Shepherds! And we're going to be singing a Christmas classic, *The First Noel,* and we encourage all those at home and in the studio to join us!

JACK: Take it away, Shepherds!

[Audio or live version of The First Noel is sung. If the production is smaller and the same kids rotate between bands, all the cast can sing the carol. If there are different kids for each band

have the kids onstage sing and the audience join in to help with volume.

Song ends. Allow time for applause.]

JACK: Wow, that was great!

SHEPHERD 2: Thank you! We've been practicing that song for a while.

HAPPY *(doing his best to play along)*: So… where does your group come from?

SHEPHERD 3 *(with a big, mischievous grin)*: Oh, you know, just your various hills and fields.

HAPPY: Wait a minute. You're actually real-life shepherds?

SHEPHERD 1: Sure! Day in and day out we tend our sheep and enjoy the beauty of God's creation. It was a simple life.

JACK *(thoroughly interested)*: What do you mean 'was'?

SHEPHERD 2: You'll never guess! We had a visitor a few days ago who inspired us to become a band. An angel appeared to us, and the glory of God shone all around us!

SHEEP 1: It was really scary!

SHEPHERD 3: But the angel told us not to be afraid and that they had joyful news for everyone! They said that a Savior had been born and he was the Messiah we had been waiting for. If we went to Bethlehem, we would find him wrapped up in cloth and lying in a manger!

SHEPHERD 1: So we went to find him! And we've been singing and telling people about it ever since!

SHEEP 2: We thought we would come and tell all the people who listen on the radio and spread the good news!

HAPPY: Hang on. You're saying you're the *actual* shepherds from the Nativity story?

SHEPHERD 2: That's right!

HAPPY *(doubtfully)*: How is that even possible?

SHEPHERD 3: We figured some people just haven't heard the story yet. Or need a little sign of hope. Jesus, the baby born in Bethlehem, is hope!

[THE SIMPLE SHEPHERDS and JACK look at HAPPY'S scowling face and are concerned.]

SHEPHERD 3 *(cont'd.)*: You look like you could use some hope, Mr. Highmore.

HAPPY *(scowling harder)*: I'm fine. I'm just not in the mood for Christmas.

JACK *(attempting to keep the peace)*: Uh... Well, that was The Simple Shepherds, folks! Thanks for stopping by!

SHEEP 1: No problem!

SHEEP 2: Bye, Mr. Highmore!

[THE SIMPLE SHEPHERDS exit. HAPPY has doubled down on his grumpiness and stands behind his microphone with arms folded.]

SCENE THREE

"A KING CHANGES EVERYTHING"

[JACK looks at HAPPY for a moment, shrugs, and signals AD. MAN to change the poster to Eastern Coffeehouse, a coffee company.]

JACK: And now another word from our sponsors! We here at STAR Radio are up all night, bringing you the best Christmas music. But we need some fuel to keep us going. That's why we drink Eastern Coffeehouse coffee. Just the sound of the coffee hitting the mug is enough to wake someone up. **[SFX: Coffee pouring.]** So, whether you're up at the crack of dawn, **[SFX: Rooster crow.]** or a night owl who is chasing the stars, **[SFX: Owl hoot.]** choose Eastern Coffeehouse coffee as your fuel of choice! **[SFX: Sip and "aah"!]**

JACK *(cheerily, as usual)*: Well, Hap, how are you feeling?

HAPPY (*frowning severely*): About the same, Jack. None of this show makes any sense. And working on Christmas Eve tends to put a damper on my mood.

JACK: Not for me! I think it's great getting to spend my holiday cheering up the masses with delightful Christmas music!

HAPPY: That makes one of us.

JACK (*clapping Happy on the shoulder*): Maybe you'll feel better after listening to our next guests, Kings and Camels! **[SFX: Applause.]**

[KINGS AND CAMELS enter in full rock and roll get up, along with five GIFT BEARERS carrying festively wrapped gifts of many sizes, including a very large box carried by two of them. (GIFT BEARERS can be in toned down rock and roll gear or regular dress clothes.) Many rock and roll instruments are along for the ride: an electric guitar, bass guitar, maybe a keytar if someone's feeling creative. The three band members are stoic looking and tough.

JACK nods encouragingly at HAPPY who reluctantly steps up to the microphone.]

HAPPY (*less than enthusiastic*): Welcome to STAR Radio.

KING 1 (*sternly*): Thank you. We're delighted to be here.

HAPPY: Finally. Someone who isn't in the mood for Christmas!

JACK *(startled)*: Sure doesn't look like you're delighted.

KING 2 *(seriously)*: Kings are very important people. We can't just be smiling and running around all willy nilly.

JACK *(eyeing their get-up)*: Oh... Alright. What will you be singing?

KING 3 *(deadpan)*: Isn't it obvious?

[Audio or live version of We Three Kings is sung. A use of drums or percussion would be fun. See note from The First Noel regarding who will sing.

Song ends. Allow time for applause.]

JACK *(impressed)*: Wow, great job! That was really good!

KING 1: Thank you. We have traveled a very long way to get to your show. This STAR Radio.

HAPPY *(who has had just about enough)*: Ha, ha, ha. Very funny. Three kings following a star with presents in tow. Let me guess, you're the kings from the nativity story, too, huh?

KING 2 *(unsure why Happy is upset)*: That is correct. We woke up one evening to a blinding light. Turns out it was a massive star. So, we decided to follow it. Something so big and bright must be important.

KING 3: We read a *lot* of old prophecies and scriptures and discovered that it was the sign of Jesus the Messiah's coming.

So, we packed our bags and brought along some gifts for the true king.

KING 1: Then we were in for a surprise. We got called to Herod's palace and he was not happy. And an unhappy king is *not* a laughing matter.

JACK *(sarcastically)*: Is anything a laughing matter to you?

KING 2: No.

[KING 2 stares at JACK sternly until JACK holds up his hands in defeat.]

KING 2: As I was saying, we went to Herod's palace, and he told us to give him all the information we had on Jesus. Herod is an intimidating guy, so we agreed and continued our travels.

KING 3 *(a little awe and excitement breaking through his stoicism)*: But once we saw the Messiah lying in a manger, we immediately fell at his feet and worshiped him. We gave our gifts of gold, frankincense, and myrrh.

JACK: That sounds like one impressive baby.

KING 1 *(smiling a little)*: He is. That was the first time I had smiled in years.

JACK *(intrigued)*: What about this Herod guy? He sounds like trouble.

KING 2 *(also giving a small smile)*: Indeed. We had a dream and an angel warned us not to return to his palace. We decided to take the long way home and deliver presents and the good news of Jesus to everyone!

KING 3: We even have a present for you, Mr. Highmore, for letting us be on your show. The knowledge that Jesus had arrived on earth was enough to break our serious mood. We hope this gift is a reminder to you that Jesus has come to bring peace on earth and goodwill to all men.

[KINGS gesture to the GIFT BEARERS and they deliver a large box to HAPPY. He looks startled and unsure of what he did to deserve such a large gift.]

HAPPY: Um… thanks.

[There is a beat of silence as HAPPY stares at the present.]

HAPPY *(cont'd.)*: Hey, if you're really the Kings and Camels, where are the camels?

KING 1 *(back to being serious)*: Outside. Having a two-humped camel means we're double parked. **[SFX: Drum sound that accompanies the end of a bad joke (bad-dum-tss).]**

KINGS AND GIFT BEARERS: Have a Merry Christmas!

[KINGS AND CAMELS exit.

JACK, SFX, CBO, and AD. MAN. are chuckling over the joke. HAPPY'S eyes are glued to the present. He doesn't open it, but the audience can tell he wants to.

JACK notices his hesitation, smiles kindly, and signals the CBO to break for intermission.]

JACK: Well, ladies and gents, I think it's time we take an intermission. Not to worry, though! We'll be right back after this musical interlude!

[A beat of silence as the CBO fiddles with the sound board and switches off the ON AIR sign.]

CBO: And we're out!

INTERMISSION

['Intermission' can take as long as you like, featuring one or two musical numbers from kids who are interested in playing some music.

While the musical guests are playing, JACK sits down and reads a paper/drinks coffee. SFX, CBO, and AD. MAN. can be getting ready quietly for the next act.

Alternatively, all CAST (except HAPPY) can join the church choir for an Advent-themed anthem.

During the music HAPPY moves the present to his desk and sits in his chair staring at the gift and listening interestedly.]

SCENE ONE

"HARK! A TURNING POINT!"

[When the music ends, hold for applause. JACK, SFX, CBO, and AD. MAN. take their places. CBO flicks three, two, one with their fingers and turns on the ON AIR sign.]

JACK: And we're back! We're heading down the home stretch, folks! One final word from our sponsors.

[AD. MAN. reveals a poster for Gurgle Guard, an antacid company.]

JACK *(cont'd.)*: Tomorrow's Christmas day and we all know what that means! FOOD. The biggest Christmas dinner you ever did eat. And who will be your fixer when you eat too much? Gurgle Guard! Just drop two of their pink disks into a glass of water, **[SFX: Drop two quarters into a glass of water, or the sound of pop fizzing in glass.]** let them dissolve and get back to stuffing your face with turkey! **[SFX: "Mmm!"]**

[HAPPY is still sitting in his chair and JACK waves him over to the microphones.]

JACK *(cont'd.)*: You ready for our final guest, Happy?

HAPPY *(a little lost)*: I guess so. I'm feeling a little confused.

JACK *(smiling encouragingly)*: Alrighty! Let's give a big STAR Radio welcome to The Little Angel Band! **[SFX: Applause.]**

[THE LITTLE ANGEL BAND enters decked out in white and gold. A hand-held harp or two can be present, but it should be all about the voices! They are all smiles and joy!]

ANGEL 1 *(enthusiastically)*: Hello! We're The Little Angel Band!

ANGEL 2: And we've come to sing songs of great joy!

[Audio or live version of Angels We Have Heard on High. Lush piano or string accompaniment. See note from The First Noel regarding who will sing.

Song ends. Allow time for applause.]

JACK *(a little misty-eyed)*: That was beautiful! What do you think, Hap?

HAPPY *(equally moved)*: Yeah, it was.

ANGEL 3: Thank you! We've been singing it all over the place. To shepherds, kings, and most recently, to the entire city of Bethlehem at Jesus' birth!

JACK: Wow, that's a big audience! What did you say to them?

ANGEL 4 *(with great joy)*: Glory to God in the highest heaven, and on earth peace to those on whom his favor rests!

[HAPPY throws up his hands.]

HAPPY *(extremely frustrated)*: That's great and all, but how can you be so joyous? It seems like every guest on this show has a place to go for Christmas to experience something wonderful, but I'm stuck here! I'm all alone in this old radio station.

ANGEL 1 *(sympathetically)*: Mr. Highmore, you're not alone! Jesus came to earth so that we could have a friend forever.

ANGEL 2: And you may not be in a warm home right now, but neither was Jesus when he was born.

HAPPY *(skeptically)*: Really?

ANGEL 3: Open your present and see!

[HAPPY moves over to his desk and opens the present. Slowly, he takes out individual figures that make up a Nativity set, complete with stable. As he arranges them, he becomes overwhelmed with emotion as the ANGELS keep speaking.]

ANGEL 4: Jesus was born in a stable; a cold place full of animals and hay.

ANGEL 1: But there was so much love in that tiny barn, it didn't matter.

ANGEL 2: Jesus' true home is in your heart, Mr. Highmore. And when he is with you, you'll never be lonely!

[HAPPY picks up the figurine of Jesus and looks at it wondrously, amazed that such a small person could hold so much meaning. He wanders back over to his microphone.]

HAPPY: I've never thought about that before. Thank you.

[JACK grins at his boss and claps a hand on his shoulder.]

JACK: Well, Little Angel Band? How about one more song for the road?

ANGEL 4 *(excitedly)*: Sure, we'll sing one of our favorites!

[Audio or live version of Joy to the World is sung. As big and joyful as possible; perhaps using an organ to accompany the cast and audience's singing. For this carol, have all the cast come out and sing along. The fuller the stage, the better.

During the last verse and refrain, HAPPY, all smiles now, wanders over to his desk chair and returns baby Jesus to the nativity. After a moment of watching the singers, he nods off again.

Song ends. Allow time for applause.

*All cast leaves including Jack, SFX, CBO, and AD. MAN.
Make sure to take the remnants of the present wrapping, roster
board, and commercial posters as everyone exits, but leave the
Nativity. ON AIR sign stays lit.]*

SCENE TWO

"WHAT DAY IS IT?"

[Another Christmas crooner classic fades in as HAPPY snores lightly. After a moment he jerks awake looking around for proof of what had happened. After a while he shakes his head, content to believe he dreamed the whole episode.

Song fades out.]

HAPPY *(rubbing his eyes)*: Woah! That was some dream!

[His eyes fall on the remaining Nativity scene on his desk, and he smiles to himself.]

HAPPY: Or maybe not…

[JACK enters, this time with a hat and coat on.]

JACK *(kind, but teasingly)*: Hey, boss! Thought I might find you here! Did I catch you sleeping on the job?

HAPPY *(chuckling)*: Actually, you did! Hey, what day is it?

JACK *(grinning)*: It's Christmas Day, Hap. Want to come celebrate with my family?

HAPPY: Sure! Just let me sign off.

[JACK leaves with a wave and HAPPY picks up the Jesus figure and looks at it for a moment before placing it in his pocket. He approaches his microphone with renewed enthusiasm.]

HAPPY *(cont'd. to audience)*: There you have it, ladies and gentlemen. Three amazing musical acts and I feel like a changed man! I hope you experienced as much hope, peace, and love as I certainly did. It will be a lesson to remember for a lifetime. This is Happy Highmore signing off. Merry Christmas!

[HAPPY wanders over, fiddles with the control board, switches off the ON AIR sign, dons his hat and coat and leaves.

If possible, have the lights dim in time with HAPPY leaving.]

END OF SHOW

Scene and Character Breakdown

ACT ONE

PROLOGUE
Setting: Performance Space, Real Time
Characters: Happy

SCENE ONE: BAA HUMBUG
Setting: Performance Space, Dream World
Characters: Happy, Jack, SFX, CBO, Ad. Man., The Simple Shepherds

SCENE TWO: A KING CHANGES EVERYTHING
Setting: Performance Space, Dream World
Characters: Happy, Jack, SFX, CBO, Ad. Man., Kings and Camels, Gift Bearers

ACT TWO

SCENE ONE: HARK! A TURNING POINT!
Setting: Performance Space, Dream World

Characters: Happy, Jack, SFX, SBO, Ad. Man., The Little
Angel Band, all remaining Cast.

SCENE TWO: WHAT DAY IS IT?

Setting: Performance Space, Real Time
Characters: Happy, Jack

PRODUCTION NOTES

STAGING OPTIONS: This production has been successfully
performed on a relatively small stage to an entire sanctuary.
Don't be shy with playing around with staging. Utilize
the space allotted for the production creatively. Consider
having all musical guests process in from the back of the
space. Have fun with the usual AV people and let the kids
takeover the booth. Ultimately, the feel of the space should
be a combination of cozy and cluttered with distinct places
for each radio station worker: Happy and Jack's desk area, the
control booth, the sound effects table, the performance area
for the musical guests, and Happy and Jack's hosting spots.

One of the most important things about any staging
decision for this show is making sure microphones are easily
accessible. Especially for the sound effects booth and the
two hosts. Make sure access to microphones is a top priority
when deciding staging.

LINE AND CHARACTER CHANGES: This show
is relatively small, but can be adapted so it fits groups of
different sizes. Consider having more than one co-host and
split up Jack's parts. Have another cast member do the
announcing for the commercials besides Jack. For those who
work specifically with curriculum or youth programming,

feel free to add mention to any Advent or yearly lesson youth have been working on. As this former Christian Education Director can say, with some confidence, no program or curriculum is perfect, so tailor it to suit whatever groups perform this vignette!

If a cast is smaller than the allotted parts, omitting the Gift Bearers is an easy change. Combining the SFX Artist, CBO, and Ad. Man. into one part takes some juggling, but can be done. Angel parts can be combined to a certain degree and having one or two shepherds and a single sheep is an easy way to downsize as well.

Additionally, though this show was written for two male leads, that is NOT set in stone. All that is required for the hosts is a good speaking voice and high reading comprehension. Have the musical guests become Queens and Camels (or Royalty/Rulers and Camels). There are also parts where shy children or young ones eager to share the spotlight can fill in!

Another fun addition, if space and bodies permit, would be to have a Happy 'stand-in' who remains asleep in the office chair to one side to give a reminder that he is sleeping during the dream sequence. Some fun sleights of hand/illusion could be had to switch them for the 'real' Happy before Act 2, Scene 2.

A few notes about learning lines and scripture references. Many of these parts are quite large, particularly for a youth program. Many productions have had their actors have their lines onstage with them, backed with black paper following the example of radio theatre performers. Having one or two music stands available for the hosts to have their lines on may be useful. Each of the musical guests uses a paraphrase of the NIV translation of the Bible for the retelling of the nativity story. Preferred translations may be substituted.

ADVERTISEMENTS: If the author did their job right, there should be a relatively clear nod to some very famous commercials aired during the time of this radio show. In previous productions these 'fake' commercials have been replaced with actual products and services that would have been broadcast. A little tweaking of the script and featuring these real advertisements will be a great blast from the past for any audience. For the director who likes to go all out, jingles for genuine radio and television advertisements can also be found on various music streaming services to be played before each commercial announcement.

ATMOSPHERE: To help create a cozy atmosphere for the show, try creating a playlist with Christmas carols sung by the era's artists (think Bing Crosby, Ella Fitzgerald, Dean Martin), soft jazz renditions of the classics, and a few radio jingles here and there. If this production is taking place during a worship service, collaborate with any worship leader or AV person who is usually in charge of gathering music and have the playlist play as people gather for worship and take in the stage set before them!

An actual ON AIR sign may be hard to locate. An easy DIY version has been made for previous productions by using a tall lamp, shade removed, and attaching a large cardboard box with one of the largest sides missing over the lightbulb. Cover that side with white paper, fasten black letters reading ON AIR, and cover remaining sides with black paper. A flick of the lamp switch and you have a great working sign! In most radio stations, microphones have their call sign clearly labeled. Some research into what these signs would look like during older radio shows will add a nice final touch to your set!

There are many amazing radio theatre/radio shows available, both older and current. Take some time and absorb the art to help get a feel for this vintage show!

NOTES

NOTES

NOTES

NOTES

NOTES

NOTES

NOTES

About the Author

Leigh Ellen Carson laughs as much as she writes. After a decade of designing and facilitating various ministry programs for all ages, she firmly believes that the best way to help people witness the transformative power of Jesus Christ is through laughter. Leigh has spent the past five years writing and directing her own children's plays, harnessing every kindergarten one-liner and middle schooler attempt at sarcasm to create shows that sparkle with humor and magic. In 2022 the Holy Spirit came calling and she took a step back from teaching to focus on sharing the joy of her experiences in the director's seat with the general public. Small-town ministry remains her passion and she continually strives to uphold her curriculum standard: quality over quantity. Leigh lives and writes voraciously in Conrad, Iowa. The STAR Radio Show is her first published work.

Printed in the United States
by Baker & Taylor Publisher Services